CARS AND
TRUCKS

PICTURES BY
RICHARD SCARRY

GOLDEN PRESS
Western Publishing Company, Inc.
Racine, Wisconsin

PAINTS

JACK
THE
SIGN PAINTER

GOOD LUCK
FARM

Fourteenth Printing, 1980

Tweet! goes the policeman's whistle. All the trucks stop.

Here comes the school bus! The children crowd in.

Brrr-um! The children ride off to school.

The mothers drive to the store to buy food for supper.

The grocery man and his helper carry out packages.

The gasoline truck brings gas to the service station.

"Fill her up!" says the laundry man in his truck.

The telephone is broken. Out comes the repair truck.

Repair men climb the pole. Soon the line will be fixed.

Here comes a tow truck towing a taxi. See the flat tire!

Beep! Beep! A police car and a jeep whiz by.

The coal truck dumps the coal down the chute.

Clang! Clang! The fire chief's car speeds along.

This family is taking a quiet country vacation.

Their car trailer is like a cozy little house.

Here comes the mail truck to pick up mail.

A man sells ice cream. A delivery motorcycle hurries by.

Look at the great big streamlined double-decker bus.

The big bus will travel all day and all night.

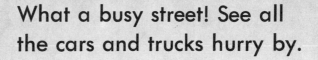

What a busy street! See all
the cars and trucks hurry by.

CHIEF
F.D.

Now all the family is going for a picnic. Goodbye!